Room Service

POEMS, MEDITATIONS, OUTCRIES

&

REMARKS

RON CARLSON

RED HEN PRESS | PASADENA, CA

Room Service

Book design by Mark E. Cull

Library of Congress Cataloging-in-Publication Data

Carlson, Ron.
  Room service : poems, meditations, outcries & remarks / Ron Carlson.—1st ed.
    p. cm.
  ISBN 978-1-59709-233-3
  I. Title.
  PS3553.A733R66 2012
  818'.54—dc23
                    2011041857

The Los Angeles County Arts Commission, the National Endowment for the Arts, and the Los Angeles Department of Cultural Affairs partially support Red Hen Press.

First Edition
Published by Red Hen Press
Pasadena, CA
www.redhen.org

Room Service

This book is for Michelle Latiolais and Christopher Merrill

ACKNOWLEDGMENTS

PERIODICALS

Camas, "Say Hello to Copper Bob"; *Chautauqua Journal,* "Under Heaven at the Utah Cabin, July 3"; *Esquire,* "Pennies," "Max Who Caught a Car," "The Great Open Mouth Anti-Sadness"; *Faultline,* "My America Notwithstanding," "My America House Car Store," "My America Coffee"; *Flash Fiction,* "A Brown Dog Sleeps on a Rag Rug"; *Fourteen Hills,* "Poetry's Debt to Invention," "Rain"; *Hayden's Ferry Review,* "Time of Day," "How Death is Not a Thing"; *The Hotchkiss Review,* "What I did not teach you about poetry"; *Hunger Mountain,* "The Bull"; *Ironhorse Review,* "Don and Hugh"; *Juked,* "The Chance"; *L Magazine,* "Homeschool Insider: the Fighting Pterodactyls"; *The Los Angeles Times,* "The Chapman Branch"; *Mississippi Review,* "Grief"; *My Weekly Reader,* "Max Who Caught a Car"; *Ninth Letter,* "My America Sleep"; *Ploughshares,* "In the Old Firehouse"; *Santa Monica Review,* "After the Animal Fair"; *Washington Post Magazine,* "Remarks to the Graduating Class"; *Washington Square,* "How to Win her Heart," "Syllabus"; *Witness,* "There were Two of Them in the Car"; *The Yalobusha Review,* "The Gunslinger's Lamentation"; *Zocalo.com,* "The Genius of Women's Wear," "Zebra."

ANTHOLOGIES

The Manner of the Country, (Univ. of Texas Press), "Under Heaven at the Utah Cabin, July 3"; *Fresh Flash; Short Short Stories about Youth* (Persea Books), "Homeschool Insider: the Fighting Pterodactyls"; *Mid American Review, Flash Fiction* (WW Norton), "The Great Open Mouth Anti-Sadness"; *Unleashed: Poems by Writers' Dogs* (Crown), "Max Who Caught a Car."

CONTENTS

I.

II.

III.

Part I

The person who labored over the *Book of Love* spent years researching love and then decades looking at *of*.

I want to live my life immediately.

—Bill K.

Room Service

We called room service, just to see, and they sent up a room, and it was good so we ordered another, this time with a view and it was lovely and there was plenty of, well, room, I mean this was light and airy which is what you want sometimes, and we enjoyed it every bit, and then we wanted something small and private without a terrace and we ordered that and sat closer together which was very nice. By now we'd memorized the room service number and we kept dialing. We ordered a vast, cavernous room with velvet walls and chandeliers and that led us to dancing which is always a pleasure. We ordered a room with no windows and doors and when it came it was a mystery. We ordered a glass room and classroom and a barroom and a car room. We absolutely could not stop ourselves. Room service! We ordered a showroom and we ordered a room almandine but that was crazy. We ordered garlic mashed potatoes but they didn't arrive, because this was room service not some vegetable emporium. We ordered an emporium and it was deluxe and we ordered a gymnasium and the floor there gleamed expectantly. By now it was late and we ordered a dorm room and a cloak room. Then we remembered we'd left our cloaks somewhere. The weather had changed and we'd left them on a bench or the back of a chair. We'd been out walking together, in love, and lost our cloaks, and when the cloak room arrived we held hands and cherished our history.

Poetry's Debt to Invention

Oh god what shall we put in this poem?
I know, a house; there's the bedroom
and we need the kitchen about here.
Let's put the guy in there leaning
against the counter smoking a cigarette.
People still smoke.
Now what's he thinking about?
Love? World War III? His father?
It gets tough about here.
His career? Fear? Why he seemed
To be twenty yesterday?
We're about as far as we can go
in this poem. He nears the end of
his cigarette; we don't even have
an ashtray. And what's he thinking?
What else does poetry require?
Oh, the kitchen window, of course,
and outside, oh my god, it's the ocean
breaking on the beach. We nearly forgot
the ocean.

After the wedding, drunk but not that drunk, Button lay arms-out across the bed. His tie dangled from one hand, and he wasn't surprised to feel it tugged at and then hauled suddenly away. The cat. He closed his hand. Yes, it was empty. He closed his eyes and opened his hand; then he closed his hand again and opened his eyes. Amazing the way a person is wired. He didn't need to look to know his hand was open. That tie was long gone. Button watched the ceiling fan and loved it for turning so slowly. Obviously in such slow motion it was intended only for his use for these few minutes. He worked one dress shoe off with the other, and then held it on a toe as long as he could. The air cooled his arch perfectly, and he thought that: perfect. Evaporation was such a stunning feature of life on earth. Water rises into the air. Now he opened his mouth and then a little wider than was comfortable. He tried to look, but he couldn't see. He knew his mouth was wide open. Button watched one blade of the fan take and lose a shadow as it rotated, and he wondered if opening your mouth helped you think. It seemed to be helping him. It was definitely helping him. His mind was clear. He decided to feed it a thought. His daughter was married. He'd witnessed the event this afternoon as Sharon left his arm and accepted a ring. Button decided to try another thought: She was now halfway across Dearden Bay on the way to the old Dearden Lodge. She'd be wearing her Michigan sweatshirt and jeans, and she and Larry would be leaning on the rail of the ferry's upper deck, bumping heads and talking about the lesser constellations far over Canada. Button opened his mouth a little wider; he was really thinking. And this mouth thing helped him from being sad. He wasn't sad. He was something, which was similar to sad, but his mouth and the fan and the cat and his hand and the tie, wherever it was, had helped him avoid the real sadness.

Rain

A person's crying does not sound like rain.
It is not like rain at all. Rain has its
own ten sounds, none of them like crying.
What is rain? Sometimes it's a patter.
Is crying a patter? Not to me.
Crying is like something wounded trying
to tell you where it is hidden. Or Crying
is the *wah wah wah*, you know, the real
wailing interspersed sometimes with words
like *Oh no* or *No no no* or just *wah wah*.
There are no words in the rain. There's
wind, of course, sometimes, and thunder,
but what is that saying? *Boom? Boom crash?*
So which crying and which rain sound alike,
I want to know. Oh, there's water in both;
Everybody knows that – water, water, but
it's not even the same water, and as long
as I have lived and the hours I've cried,
I've never heard a tear hit the floor.
And I was listening! I've seen tear marks
on a letter, but I didn't, and I swear this is true,
hear them hit.

A Brown Dog Sleeps on a Rag Rug

A SPOTTED DOG ENTERS THE ROOM AND CIRCLES A BROWN DOG.

Spot: You ever eat a book?

Brownie: Just don't. Don't wake a sleeping dog.

Spot: You're awake. How many books have you eaten?

Brownie: I never ate a book.

Spot: You ate a book. Every dog has eaten a book.

Brownie: One. A book. I admit it. I ate the whole book.

Spot: No you didn't. No dog ate the whole book. You ate the back binding and some of the covers where their hands had been.

Brownie: Just the binding. You're right. It was delicious.

Spot: No, it wasn't. It looked delicious, but it was dry, only slightly savory.

Brownie: It wasn't even leather. It looked like leather.

Spot: It's never leather. What was it?

Brownie: Robinson Crusoe.

Spot: That's a good book.

Brownie: It was awful. I could barely choke it down.

Spot: You cut yourself?

Brownie: Paper cuts. My tongue.

Spot: Did you also eat the Tennyson?

Brownie: I might have.

Spot: Little red book, embossed gold letters.

Brownie: Tennyson wrote more than the one book.

Spot: This was his poems about King Arthur. A red book.

Brownie: I ate it. It was better than the other book.

Spot: You ate the whole shelf.

Brownie: Oh please.

Spot: You did. Book by book. Once you'd had one, the others were easier to get at.

Brownie: Okay, they were. They fell into my mouth.

Spot: The six old volumes of Shakespeare.

Brownie: Unbelievably good. Delicious. Melted in my mouth.

Spot: It looked like it.

Brownie: I couldn't stop myself. One thing led to another. I wish he'd written more. I could use one of those books right now.

Spot: He didn't write all those plays. Christopher Marlowe, Edward de Vere . . .

Brownie: Shakespeare wrote those books.

Spot: Ben Johnson, Queen Elizabeth, William Stanley who was the Earl of Derby.

Brownie: In that case, I never had a book in my mouth. I haven't. I've been sleeping and you came in from the library. I'm an old dog who needs his sleep. I saw the books on the floor in there and they made me tired and so I came in here hours ago. I've never even licked a book. The Earl of Derby! I wouldn't know a book from a hole in the ground. Well, I'd know a hole in the ground, but I had nothing to do with any of those either. Mainly, I've been sleeping and then you came in and wanted to talk.

Time of Day

What we want is a way through
all this lawn furniture. Even now
down in the mystery thicket
men ride mowers all night long.
My sleep is full of nickels.
Oh god, sit with me on the stone step.
My wife is inside smiling.
My children are famous. One
built the Globe Theatre. Maybe
you've heard of it. The other
burned it down. I started our
genealogy but it was like
reading the papers. All my projects
are in tatters, I mean, under option.
Here comes the sun and the hard
part. We'd better face it: though
we love our coffee, it isn't
morning around here anymore.

PENNIES

There were pennies in the urinals by midnight
which meant Armando was somewhere in the bar.
It changed my heart badly to see them. I had been
dancing with Caitlin very skillfully and now I was
only looking forward to the back door.
My buddy Vernon found me and said,
"You're out of here. I seen him."
Summer was over. Everybody knew the warning
and avoided pennies all over town. It was better to overpay
than get involved with copper coins. I walked the
gravel parking lot alone hoping my truck windows
weren't broken. It was cold and tonight would try for first frost.
I'm not alone in this: hating change.

How Death is Not a Thing

or a person or a place
to be spotted at an intersection,
"There it is," we might say,
waiting for the WALK sign.
or somewhere else, we see death
approaching like a friend
all teeth and how-de-do?
No way. No death was over there
or over there. Or there was death
smelling like death. Wrong.
That's not death. That smell
is bacteria by the jillions at
the next festival, the biggest
small party in the world.
And none of this death
was this shape or anything
about the shadow of death,
how it fell across this or that.
It has no shadow. Light falls
everywhere, cut by real things
at different times of day, such as
that apple tree on Route 41
just after noon
that spring so long ago.

for Danny Fritz

GRIEF

The King died. Long live the King. Then the Queen died. She was buried beside him. The King died and then the Queen died of grief. This was the posted report. And no one said a thing. But you can't die of grief. It can take away your appetite and keep you in your chamber, but not forever. It isn't terminal. Time works on it and eventually you'll come out and want a toddy. The Queen died subsequent to the King, but not of grief. I know the Royal Coroner, have seen him around, a young guy with a good job. The death rate for royalty is so much lower that that of the general populace. He was summoned by the musicians, and he found her on the bedroom floor, checked for a pulse, and wrote, "Grief" on the royal form. It looked good. And it was necessary. It answered the thousand questions about the state of the nation. He didn't examine the body, perform an autopsy. If he had, he wouldn't have found grief. There is no place for grief in the body. He would have found a blood alcohol level of one point nine and he would have found a clot of improperly chewed tangerine in the lady's throat which she ingested while laughing. But this seems a fine point. The Queen is dead. Long live her grief. Long live the Duke of Reddington and the Earl of Halstar who were with me that night entertaining the Queen in her chambers. She was a vigorous sort. And long live the posted report which will always fill a royal place in this old kingdom.

HOMESCHOOL INSIDER: THE FIGHTING PTERODACTYLS

When we finally decided on homeschool for my sister Joylene and me, our first challenge was to select a mascot. After all, I'd been a Cougar at Big River Elementary and Joylene had been a Leopard at the high school, and now at our house who were we? We settled on the Fighting Pterodactyls, because it sounded terrific and used one of my spelling words. But there was something sad about knowing we didn't exactly have any rival schools. The Rubynars have homeschooling and so we did go over to their house and tell them they were our rival school, but it wasn't a good idea since they have seven kids and wanted to schedule a football season right away. Lloyd Rubynar chased us down the street with Joylene insulting him all the way, asking what was their mascot, what were their school colors, why don't they clean up their campus, things like that, things Lloyd would have a little trouble with.

I asked Joylene what our school colors were and she said, green and green, after our Plymouth and the color of our fridge which is avocado, another spelling word.

Then, right off the bat during our first semester of homeschool, Joylene lost the hall pass. She'd already lost the livingroom pass, the garage pass, and the yard pass. Our teacher, Mrs. Yollstrom (our mother) put her in detention, and we both were unable to leave the kitchen table all day long. "I don't want you wandering the hallway without a pass," Mrs. Yollstrom told us. Mrs. Yollstrom's brother, Uncle-Todd, was on the couch as he had been for the two years that he's been under house arrest, sitting there with that little deal locked around his ankle, and Mrs. Yollstrom pointed at him as she had plenty of times before and said, "Do you want to end up like Todd? He didn't have a hallpass either!" She said we could earn it back by cleaning up the campus, which meant Joylene mowed the backyard and I swept the patio. It's a lovely campus in the fall with the sycamore leaves turning, the two old boats against the back fence, and the students (me and Joylene) strolling around with rakes and brooms.

So many things are the same here in homeschool as they were at Big River. There's no talking and you've got to keep your eyes on your own paper. From time to time I'll accidentally put a book report over a butter stain and grease it up pretty good, but Mrs. Yollstrom doesn't take points off for food marks. And if you're caught chewing gum, you have to spit it out or give some to the whole class, which is a good deal here since it's just the one other piece.

The Pterodactyl Green on Green Junior Prom was a big disappointment for Joylene, but she shouldn't have got her hopes up. We had the a.m. radio in the den and big bowls of Doritos and we turned the lights down, but it wasn't too interesting. I'm in fifth grade and I don't dance. Mrs. Yollstrom was there as chaperone, standing in the corner. Uncle Todd wanted to dance, but Mrs. Yollstrom didn't allow it. There's a firm school policy about jailbirds. We finally just turned on "Matlock," and Joylene cried quietly for a while which was kind of like the prom anyway. She looked sweet in her green satin dress.

At the beginning of spring semester our brother Dean dropped out of Cornell and returned home to pursue his post graduate work at the other end of the kitchen table. He said homeschool was a natural for him. "There the tuition was crushing and I was looking for a smaller school anyway," he said. But he is worried that his doctorate in paleontology is going to take him longer here with us Pterodactyls because Dad has to spend so much time at the boat shop that Dean might not get all the quality tutorial and thesis and lab work he needs. It's fun to have him home though – all our family together: Uncle Todd over on the couch in house arrest, Dean down the table in graduate school, Joylene next to me in high school, and me in my chair studying fractions and Cuba with Mrs. Yollstrom, and learning the social skills necessary to survive in higher and higher education.

There Were Two of Them in the Car

There was some legitimate confusion about what
had happened along the old reservoir the last
June night in the Twentieth Century, but now
we have learned what happened by using big
shovels and brooms: Archaeology! We have dug down
through the ages and we have the evidence!
There were two of them in the car
frozen in time for all of eternity
in positions which were revealing! The Woman
whom we have discovered was driving had her hands
on the wheel. It took weeks to unearth her using
vacuums and spectroscopes and the like! We
were careful! Her expression is serious and somewhat
tender. Human beings were tender! We've learned so much!
The Man was harder to uncover, but we were stubborn.
We dug for months and brushed him off with a big brush!
His face! Let's just say he was confused! And we know
from the texture of the earth we brushed from
the surface of his eyes, that there was moisture there.
Human beings had water in
their eyes – some of the men! But this guy had something
else. His mouth was open and then we got real careful with
our archaeology. Imagine! He'd been talking! He was
a talker! We were onto something,
something deep and secret which will exist for all time!
What we did is we took the earth from his open mouth and
examined it using big technical devices and complicated
scientific machines. This required all our concentration!
We were perplexed by our findings.
The material was spread out on our lighted table.

It spelled out some word, a code.
LOVE was the word. We'd taken it straight from his
mouth. We gathered round the bright table and looked at it
all night. LOVE? Finally our work was at an end. The word
was a rocky puzzle. We sent somebody
to look it up.

Class Remarks

My fellow students. Time's winged chariot heads our way loaded down with the complexities of our demanding future, and I'd like to meet the challenges of tomorrow fully prepared and not encumbered by the quaint instruments of yesterday. I don't feel encumbered, but how do you ever know? If the goal is to be cumbered; bring it on.

It behooves us now to download our manifest duties. So many things are behooving us, it's a little daunting. But be not daunted. Everybody at one time or another gets behooved real good, and most folks come out of it O.K.

Today we are the edge of a bright new tomorrow, but we don't know which edge. I say: carpe diem. In fact, I say take two, they're small. Who among us seeks to fulfill his or her potential? Let us get in line with our shoulders to the wheel when we find a wheel that fits, looks good, and has benefits up the wazoo. Excuse my language, but the time for hesitation might be through.

This is Commencement which we all know means making room in your backpack for the demands of our complex tomorrows. Get real, did you think they would call this Termination. And I'm going to miss this place. I for one liked the dress code, but those books were heavy. And I didn't understand everything the faculty was saying, and they said plenty. I burned some midnight oil, at least that's what I think it was, and we passed through the dark night of something to the end of the day. At the end of the day, of course, it's night again. What I'm saying is time has passed.

So now we must meet the burning questions of the modern world of tomorrow For some reason these questions are on fire. God knows, we did some stuff, but we didn't light up any questions that I know of. We were kids, doing what we were told some of the time, and then suddenly here we are and we're looking at the questions that happen to be in flames.

One question that keeps coming up is: Why did the residents of Skull Island build a wall to protect themselves from King Kong, and then make a door in the wall big enough for him to walk through? Is this what we've just done by studying so hard? Have we built a big door in a big wall? Can our King Kong walk through and get us? The future wants us really bad. It's looking over the wall right now. When it finds that door, the next thing will happen. It always does.

Hey, what am I talking about? This is a day of joyous celebration. We should be happy. We have strived to get here through thick and thin. Who knew striving would be this hard and involve so many pizzas? We strove in the dorms and on the commons, and by dint of our striving we have emerged into the real world. I expect we'll need more dint out here.

We are the newest citizens of the modern real world of tomorrow, and let us try to take the path less traveled while marching a mile to the different drummer in someone else's shoes. Something has been bestowed upon us, can you feel it? It's a little like freaking out. The future waits for no man. The future waits for no woman. I get the impression the future won't wait. Here, suddenly is the future with its big teeth, and us such tender morsels.

ONE WOMAN

Oh, the old love song again and again
devotion and desire without end,
a woman half dressed somewhere and
being admired, or dressed and being admired.

These men go off alone into their rooms
and write it down: she was this and she was that.
Every man says she's the woman above all,
on a pedestal, though no one says pedestal,
that would be crazy,
and there's a thousand of these poems,
and by that I mean a million declarations
of this singular love of this one of a kind woman,
so rare, an absolute phenomenon which
many times rivals the moon or the oceans,
or the wind in the trees or night or any of the
furniture of night or day.

You see what I mean:
big unknowable things.
What are we to make of it? This:
it's true. Each man is telling the truth.
Each woman puts all the other women second.
It's the way. The strap of her gown off her shoulder,
and the paradox prevails. These poems are
all true. Each woman stands alone
in the doorway or on the pedestal
in the perfect light.

Today is Insect Day in this world, and the sun has invented all of these creatures who now work ceaselessly in the grasses and trees surrounding the cabin: the bees, ten kinds of bees, some who whistle or is it sizzle as they bump against the eaves in some kind of labor; and the flies, twenty kinds, some very small who still retain the ability to bite, and the gorgeous and feared horsefly on my shoelaces, standing there in twenty blinking facets, rubbing her forearms together as if rolling up her sleeves for the duties to come; and the little beetles, narrow as exclamation points, but less excited; and the one hornet all alone dragging his golden quotation mark legs through the air looking for a mate so they could quote something; and the butterflies through whose wings the sun shines completely, orange and brown, and flying in hiccups or so it seems to the inept human observer. The sun doesn't shine through many parts of his human body, maybe the shellbacks of the ears, but it doesn't shine through his ribcage, which he so desires. The trillion ants are imperturbable; they don't act like it is crowded, and the glistening black ants walk around like dogs, some of them wearing leashes and shiny colors. When the human spilled grape jam on the kitchen counter, suddenly there was a black ant. He'd found the motherlode and he nosed the jam and then circled the sink to tell his three buddies back by the wall. The human interrupted their plan, and when he swiped them carefully up in a paper towel, they came popping out of it with a skill that goes back a millennium, survivors, but they were escorted thus quickly to the front lawn. Certainly they regathered there, all four, and the three asked the one with a purple mouth: what did it taste like? Is it really good? The human knows that he will see them again. And there is the little quick gray spider in the bathtub who always comes out when the human appears; the gray spider wants to see who's messing, and who the hell cleaned up all the flies? Does the human think he killed them for nothing? He's late for lunch.

It is a day of insects, but a human being needs to stand still to see them. To look at the ground is to see a cosmos in motion; there's an ant climbing a long blade of grass, three inches, and then disappointed at the top, he climbs down. He thought this elevator went to the tenth floor. He hoped actually it went up to the hummingbird feeder from which the drop of sugar he'd chased had fallen. On hands and knees, the human can raise his gigantic head and see the far hills, imbedded with red rocks like jewels in a crazy present for the king, and between where his hands rest in the dirt and those rocks there are unlimited creatures blessing the earth, uncountable motions in brief lives, and the human wishes with his human heart, which is an imprecise instrument, that he could find god here, that god would appear. But he may have. The human heart may not be the right tool for the job. It's like trying to paint a picture with a drum. Or something. The human knows he loves this world, and that his sadness is a blessing of some kind which will either be revealed to him or not, but he will use the days to breath and to call himself to mindfulness, some of the time.

The Genius of Women's Wear

Uncertainty roams the city freely, unchecked by traffic rules or time of day, making itself at home everywhere, even in the big houses and the small houses and the places of commerce and trade, and it can winnow into the smallest places, the left ventricle and the right ventricle, any ventricle it chooses, all of them really, and it can perch heavily on me, god knows, and has become my sidekick and steady partner, like a little guy in a red suit on my shoulder with a pitchfork or trident, some wicked tool, whispering his pernicious questions all the livelong day, and until I met you, I thought he was here to stay.

But when you came to the door in your underwear holding two dresses before you on hangers, and you asked me, which one you should wear, I knew everything I needed to know. I am going to get you more dresses and more hangers for all the days to come, all the sweet certain days. I know now that you have made a choice, and that I, who knew nothing about apparel am now the genius of women's wear and will be forevermore.

The Gunslinger's Lamentation

When it's twilight in a town like this and the street glows and the horses whisper or seem to whisper and the big cottonwoods behind the mercantile begin to whisper or seem to whisper and the creek along side the livery stable whispers and it is whispering certainly, then I always get a hankering to put down my guns for good, and all the ways of the gun which have run me so long, and stay in this sweet place when the other gunslingers in my outfit ride on in the morning. I'm always tired when this hankering comes on and thirsty and I start thinking about putting a boot up on the bar down the street and sanding off the corners of my throat with some bitter rye whiskey which is a hard medicine, but my medicine all these years. The hankering is a real hankering and I'll talk about it. My guns are heavy, and the leather belt, one I had made outside of El Paso with an ornate stitchery in heavy golden saddle thread which makes a long loop of sunflowers along the whole thing, is also heavy, always wet with sweat and always every minute of every day filled with thirty-six thirty caliber pistol cartridges which bear their own weight. My guns are not twins except that they each weight plenty, the two revolving barrels coated with silver and nickel and the grips being polished antelope prong and simply ivory in the one I mainly use. I don't need to carry two guns night and day, but it has been shown to me that with two I have to use one less often. Two guns form a more ponderous threshold between me and the trouble which has been a steady feature of my life; but regardless of how formidable a threshold, it is in a doorway, and trouble enters in. So at the end of the day, with my collar button open for what all might be, my gun belt chafes at me as if to scold me for the choices that I've made, and carrying this load down three or four or five doors to the drink hall or saloon, I am visited by a hankering to step into any alley in the town and unclip all four buckles on the belt and set it slowly against the dark building there and walk away lighter and absolutely free.

The hankering goes on. I hanker to stay here and have the longest breakfast in the west, eating bacon and eggs and drinking coffee in the café until I knew the name of every citizen of this town and where they lived and where I might find a little piece of land with some low hills and trees and a small part of a river, a place I might raise some cattle for whatever purposes cattle are put, and build a house with a porch and paint that, the whole thing: porch house and rail. There'd be a rail. I hanker to sit there in the evenings in some chair I'd obtain and when I stand up I'd step down off the porch and put my hand into the air and feel tomorrow's weather and know thereby what plans to make. After the cattle industry developed and thrived, I also would have fulfilled my hankering for a heavy gauge rail line to haul people and supplies (including some of those cattle) across the whole country. A thousand miles of steel track with the sidings and necessary maintenance facilities. I'd hanker to get married and I'd marry a pretty woman who was also strong and smarter than me which includes almost all women, and I'd hanker to marry a woman who was a steamboat captain and together we'd invest in her boat, a three decker paddle wheel called The Seven Seas, and on that ship we'd tour the great rivers top to bottom and offer travelers rare luxury such as golden brocade chairs with ottomans and reading lamps for the leather books of history on the walnut bookshelves. I'd hanker to meet the great politicians and soldiers and artists who could afford such travel and my wife and I would enchant them at the captain's table and advise them on issues of state and how to apportion the resources of the country and where the borders of the states might best be placed. In all we'd have nine such steamships and employ the thousand men and women necessary to their continued service, jobs with benefits and the chance to do some good in the larger world. My hankering would include of course children, probably eight children, a bona fide legacy, who would grow up learning to spell correctly and how to settle disputes with reason and goodwill, and each of whom would learn a trade or an art and find room to practice it. I'd hanker for piano, probably a couple of pianos, and my children would play the pianos.

The sound of a piano in the twilight when you don't know the location of the piano is a plaintive sound indeed, regardless if it is a rollicking tune, as they are called, or one of the great dead composer's sonatas, and some nights as I walk back in the new dark toward the saloon, as it is called in stories, the piano wants to pull at me until I do peel off these old guns. Too many nights, the pearl handled pistol is still warm from work and it can be a biting heat reminiscent of the harm accomplished. It is a world of harm and I am a citizen thereof. But I'm a professional, if anything, and I can withstand an onslaught of heat and of the hurtful musical notes and all of the hankering they engender, and I understand with a clarity as solid as the weight of my gun belt, that I'm going to have a couple three rocky drinks and feel them burn a warm place in my breast for a minute which will have to serve as the only good thing in the life I have chosen.

Anaconda, a Giant Invader

Everybody knew the anaconda lived in Dark Lake. Or it lived in the jungle. It lived in a place that people didn't go everyday, because the anaconda, which was a giant invader, wasn't seen everyday. Our family had never been to Dark Lake; we weren't lake goers. We'd never been to Lonely Lake either. And the jungle was too far. The anaconda went months and no one saw it. They'd talk about it every week, but that was partly because the word was cool to say: anaconda. The word has a lot of meaning and what it means is giant invader. Of course it ate our house. No one had any idea that it had gotten so big it could eat a house, except the little kids who did imagine it would eat houses. What happened to us was that we came back from the bowling alley late on Sunday afternoon, because we bowled after church, and our house was gone, all the houses on our street were gone, and we found the anaconda, the giant invader, had crawled to Redwood Road and was sleeping there in the sun. We could see the exact shape of our house, even the chimney, in the stretched pattern of his skin, green and yellow. That whole section of our neighborhood was visible in the giant invader. He wasn't a threat to us sleeping there. He was full of houses. We could have gone up and touched him, if we had wanted to, but we didn't want to. Our house was right there, so close, and yet so far. For a while we thought of all the stuff in our house which was now in the snake, and then we marveled at the huge lumpy creature. How did he get so big? An anaconda doesn't get that big in nature. It's not natural. We knew that. Someone said it, and when we heard that sentiment, we knew that the anaconda had become a giant invader because of something we had done. Something with radioactivity or something with plastic bags or chemical paint stripper. Man, we did these things for years and years, and we never saw the big snake that would result. It was the story of mankind. And now we were mankind. It helped a little and it hurt a little, knowing that. We walked back to the foundation of our house. We looked in at the basement den and the bedroom down there. The bed was still made and in the den there was a red and yellow bullfighting poster on one wall we'd gotten somewhere. It was an announcement: toro this and toro that. Manuel de Palmos the great matador will do such and such on a weekend long long ago. So long ago it was impossible to imagine. You wonder if it ever happened. The days hold us in their hands like shining jewels, and our families love us in the colorful light.

Part II

He knew the Bible forward and backward and of course that was the trouble. Knowing it backward meant Jonah went home, Job grew younger and more at ease, and the whole book itself ended in the dark.

The Chance

All right, we agree, a snowball gets to hell.

We don't know how, we just know it is there,
in hell. Maybe some sinner died skiing
with a snowball in his pocket and there it is,
assuming that your clothes go to hell with you
which is a huge discussion in itself. Some bad
guy's bad heart quits while he's at the symphony
and he gets to show up in hell in a tux,
while the rest of us appear in cut off levis
and the upper half of a football jersey.

Regardless though, the snowball is in hell.
What could happen to it? A tender globe
of snow? There we are blinking in the inferno,
suddenly burning the way we knew we would,
none of us is surprised by this hot place,
the fire everywhere as promised,
and the stinging smoke almost familiar.
Forged in the instant is a certainty
that we will feed these flames forever.
Now we understand the strange phenomena-
the snowball.

      It still has a chance.

A Simple Note on How Best to Use This Humble Bookmark

First, are you sure you have come to a place in your good book where it is wise and prudent to stop reading? Couldn't you, if you really applied yourself, read on, say a page or two? How have you ascertained to stop reading? If you are in bed, are all the decisions you have made in your bed reliable decisions? Are all the decisions you have made while sleepy, truly valuable decisions? Aren't you a little skeptical of any decision you make while you are half asleep? Best would be to get out of bed and go brew some coffee while you think over your decision to use this bookmark. You can read while the coffee makes its sweet sounds in the kitchen. You've got to admit, this is a good book! When you have revived yourself enough to trust your decision-making ability, then you can properly apply this bookmark. Find the place in the book where you have finished reading, but do not put the bookmark in that place! Turn back two or three pages or four, and snug the bookmark there. Tomorrow you will have the pleasure of reading again something dear to you, something you read bravely in your kitchen with this bookmark in your hand.

could be placed in a cardboard box,
wrapped in brown paper, tied with fibered twine,
and sent through the mails to meet you at home when you arrive.
Your mother would say, as you enter that house
with your suitcase of dirty laundry and great books,
Here's a package for you, and she would pour a glass of whitecold milk.
Sit down, she'll say placing cooking on a plate with a wavy blue line
around the edge, the one you forgot about, the one you remember.
That plate, I remember that plate. And you will set down your suitcase,
a yellow sleeve caught in the side, you will set your tennis racquet
and satchel on a green wooden chair, you will sit at the table, and the table
will rise in your mind like an artifact, you will remember the wood
under your fingers. This table, I remember this, and as you set the glass
on the table in that minute your mother will say, Tell me all about it.
Your father would be settling the car in the garage you barely remember,
Dark as a dream full of lawn mowers, oil on cement, snow tires. Now
your mother, in a dress that is coming back to you now, a yellow summer dress
with vague green fish swimming around her, opens the cupboard which makes
the unique noise of wood, a soft click, I remember that sound. The water
will boil then, whistling in the light, but your only mother has decided
to have iced tea instead and stirs a glass, the way she does, saying,
Tell me all about it.   Your father will come in the screen door,
a door older than you are, these doors, you will think, are too much;
I remember them, the pennytaste of screen on your tongue. Your father
will be the man in his yard clothes. The graduate should have a beer,
he will say, selecting one from the fridge, but you forgot and already drank
the milk; your stomach is white. Strange, you don't drink milk. No,
it's all right. This is fine. Your father will be moving now; he will smell
of sun and grass clippings, the corners of his forehead will be copper.
His feet will leave tracks on the floor, and if you look down, you will
Remember the freckled beige tiles, your cheek against the cool kitchen
floor on summer days. Your mother will be up again swimming in the room,
Want a sandwich? You will not have eaten many of the cookies yet.

No, I'm fine. Your father will be the man who does not sit down. Tell us
all about it.   What you will need then as the sunlight delivers
every window in the room, every remembered fragment and artifact of yourself,
what you will need in the disturbing promise of graduation afternoon is a
sister to enter the kitchen. She will be happy for all the wrong reasons
it will seem to you: happy the refrigerator is laden with soda and beer
and colorful food, happy that school is out, and that the house smells
like one of the larger cookies in the world. Actually, she will be happy,
this sister you remember only the shadow of, because you are home smelling
of tobacco, home from a place, a school where she's never even eaten lunch,
a terminal where people say hello and get into cars or goodbye and step out of them.
She will be happy that the room is full of people she knows. Your sister
will eat the cookies.   Your mother will sit down a minute, just to sip
her clinking tea in your presence, and act which for her is enough, you are home,
and then she will be up again washing dishes that are clean, rinsing the plate.
They were good, Mom. Your father will be ready to be outdoors
now; he will go through the silverware drawer looking for an old knife
for weeding the lawn. Do I need to say you will remember the sound
of the spoons and knives being jostled, the sound of the entire drawer
as it jumps to a close? As you mother turns from the sink, her hands,
your favorite hands in the room, in all of history, still wet, you will wish
you knew what to say, some educated perfect thing. You will wish there
were a present for her somewhere in the jungle of your suitcase. But what
would it be? You've never known what to get her for a present. You won't
know that a suitcase, smelling like your own, is present enough. Now
she will be sorting your clothes onto the floor in the utility room where
the washer and dryer wait squarely. She will be saying how hard it must
have been to get clean clothes at school with all the work, and then, when
the music you clearly remember of the washer is moving through the house,
moving the house, your mother, now accustomed to the stranger in her house,
will go back across the kitchen, picking up your tennis racquet, your satchel,
then putting them down, not knowing where to put these things, and you
will think of the future, sunlight, uncut lawns, unopened mail, your room,

which is the guest room now; you will sleep in this building tonight
and with these people. Your mother will go back to the counter
by the toaster, as you wonder where you've been for a while, and she will
put one of her live hands on the brown package in her household uneasily.
This package came for you, she'll try. This package came in the mail.

The Bull

When they led me
into the China Shop
I didn't mind,
though it was a bright place
and the wooden floor creaked.
But the way they watched,
smirking at the windows
filled my bull's heart
with a sadness
so large and fragile
you could have cracked it
with a whisper.

The Chapman Branch

I've always liked what that one guy said in that one book about being able to stand up anywhere in Salt Lake City to see exactly where you are; it's an open place, held in the hands of the mountains like a big book. I grew up on the West Side across Main Street and the railroad tracks and, in fact, the river. We had to cross the river to go to our library, the Chapman Branch on Ninth West, a beautiful building full of books, and a brass bust of its benefactor, Mr. Andrew Carnegie.

My parents were readers and I read a lot of books as a kid, including that one about that guy in the frozen north and another about those guys on the island, but it was at the Chapman Branch that I read that one book where the one guy goes down the river with the other guy, and I was into this book, that is, it had established a world which I could believe in as I had no other, and then those guys meet one other guy and he is killed, and when he was killed I looked up. I remember right where I was sitting in the Chapman Branch and I remember the rectangular wooden table where I sat and the shelves of books into which I looked in the yellow library light. I knew that this was just a book, but something had come out of it for me in a way that felt too real, unfair, close. I held the book in my hands; it was that one book by that one guy. It was just a book. And the fact that it was just a book, and that I could not put it down now that this thing had happened in there, changed reading as an activity forever.

I was twelve years old and would go to Jordan Junior High School in the fall, where I would read that one real long poem by that old guy and that wicked story by that one woman where the people draw lots and a nasty paperback about that bad girl who could be mean and for no reason! That night at the Chapman Branch Library, my mother came by my table with her arms full of books for my father and little brothers; it was time to go. As we drove back across the river to our house, and now it seemed a small river, hardly as dangerous as my mother had been telling me it was for years, I didn't tell my mother that something had happened. I didn't tell her things were going fine until this one kid was killed, and that his death was a surprise to me, a surprise I was still having trouble getting over, and it was fifteen minutes later. I was in a kind of grief for that kid, a funny feeling that persisted even though I'd closed the book. I played it over in my mind, and with the sadness, I had another secret thought: how did he do that, the writer, how did he make such a book? I could see Salt Lake City laid out like a story, the capitol, the ancient spires and the towers of old downtown, the little houses starting to creep up the hillsides, and I wondered, how would one make such a book?

How to Win Her Heart

You gather everything you value and this means all the good stuff, the special things in your room, the baseball with your father's handwriting on it, for example, and your letters, those you've written by hand and typed for years, those from the living and the dead, as well as photographs and anecdotes from history, report cards, all your teachers' names, Mrs. Scanlon and Ms. Talbot and even Miss Miller and Coach Durrant, and your collections, the monster magazines, your favorite shirts and shoes, and your best remarks and moments in sport and your scars and great scratches or injuries anyway and money of course, every bit, even foreign money and every time you've been cold and every time you've been hot, and that time you fainted under the bridge in the desert, as well as the times you were hungry and all of your food certainly, butter and crackers, good crackers, and every lie you've told and how you told it, and all the dances you've danced and your favorite music, songs so important you can't even explain them, and all your terrific phone calls, good news and bad, the time you stood alone naked in the three a.m. bedroom with the phone in your hand, and your close calls, and that time in the ocean and everyone you've kissed, the first kiss and the little kisses and wrong nasty kisses and your table manners and the gaps in your understanding of mythology and grammar and any jewelry you have, even the jewelry you've received as gifts, and anything with lace or fancy buttons, and your books especially those with markings such as ink margin notes or coffee or blood and every game of Scrabble you've played, including the one true game where you tied, and fires you've started and where you've tripped and fallen down and your bicycles and your hats and caps, essentially then everything you've ever thought or had in your hand, but also to include the wind in your face as you clambered over a rocky summit and your hair stood up in that hard air, and the sight of the ocean as it approaches with its billion waves, swollen and bursting, and never the same wave twice, and include too the snow on your shoulder, even a little snow one night when you were a kid watching it snow past the streetlamp when you stared until you had vertigo and felt as if you were drifting up toward the light, your feet way off the ground, moving up with the petal snowflakes and you didn't know if you should be scared or not, but you weren't scared, and a minute later your mother pulled up in her car and set the world straight again, you got into the car with your mother. She had the radio on and the dashboard lights were glowing. Your mother picked you up. You'd been waiting outside the school winter festival, ten years old in your jacket looking up at the snow teeming by the streetlamp, and so be sure to include that red jacket and that you grew into it the next year, and put in your mother and her car and the glowing dial on the radio, always the glowing dial, and you take all of these things and you push them forward onto the big table here, push all your stuff onto one of the numbers, there are an infinite array to chose from and so choose one and put everything you value there, don't let the baseball roll away, and then look up into the bright world and say, *There now, please, spin the wheel.*

The Teeming Urban Scene

Oh ha, the crowded city teeming with its million
citizens all walking to their many destinies,
just everywhere teeming, especially
up that street and that one,
the weary throngs all teeming wearily,
endlessly teeming, even as the day
fails and evening falls on my
shoulders as I walk through the throngs,
and I am not really teeming. This is a big crowd
all right and they seem to be urban
in their teeming, and new as I am
to this populated scene, I can detect
the heartbreaking census: there is one
person missing from the millions.
If she were here, we would teem like crazy
in our perfect tiny throng.

My America House Car Store

Soldiers were dying and we heard about it, but we didn't know what it meant or what to do about it. We didn't even know how to talk about it. We didn't know if they were dying for the cause, because we didn't know the cause. Sometimes a man would comb his hair and appear on television and talk about the cause, and by the time he was finished speaking all we knew about was his hair. There was global warming and it was the same thing. Where was it? Everywhere. It was global and there was no question about the warming, but what. It was someone's fault and we'd seen the smokestacks, but evidently it was also us. Every day we drove around burning oil. We burned oil to go get our hair done and we burned oil to take the kids to soccer practice. They would practice soccer for a few years and then quit and start burning oil themselves. All day long and into the night, we burned oil and there were plenty of us doing it. We talked about ceasing burning oil, but who was going to start that? It was hard to cease because we were trained pretty hard in not ceasing. Everything in our lives told us not to cease. We were ceaseless. From time to time one of us would cease, but then sitting on the edge of the bed with our hands between our knees, we knew not what to do. We were also restless. Rest had been dwindling down for years and now there was none whatsoever. We had restless hearts and restless minds, and we had restless leg syndrome. We twitched with it sitting in our chairs because there wasn't anyplace to walk anymore. There had been a couple places to walk, but now we just walked to our cars, and they were always right there by the door. House car store. Store car house. It was hard to go back to our houses, they had betrayed us so deeply. They had been our houses for a long time and then they started growing more valuable. We'd come home and eat dinner and take a shower and go to bed and when we woke up our houses had secretly become more valuable. We wouldn't mow the lawn or paint the place and it became more valuable. They were doubling in value and then tripling in value. It was hard to see, because they were the same houses, but the value kept piling up. We thought we deserved this somehow. And still we lived in the things and threw our dirty clothes on the floor. Then these very same places where we had done one million personal things and said things out loud like we'd never said anywhere else, started to lose their value. The same houses! You couldn't do the dishes without your house losing value. House care store. Store car house. This was a period when the government was trying to get our secrets. Evidently we had a ton of secrets. I know I certainly did. Not a ton, but plenty. The government wanted our phone calls and bank records and library records. They wanted to know what books we'd checked out from the library, so they could go and read those books. I'd been reading plenty of books, and it made me feel all right to think that the government was going to do some reading. Meanwhile, we found out that the government had secrets and evidently we wanted those secrets. I'm not sure I did, but I understood our interest in finding the secret government data. It was a bitter contest to see who had the most secrets, us or the government. It was a stand off. It was a tie and we weren't talking to each other. Also we were all just full of DNA and there was DNA everywhere. The government knew our DNA and our fingerprints and our eyeball recognition, and it knew what was in our suitcases. We knew that too: it was all the same stuff. Socks. There were socks everywhere. On any day there were half a million pairs of socks in airplanes. The Wright Brothers would have been confused about that. All our socks were made in China, and they were good socks. I mean they fit. At the end of a long day of showing everybody our I.D.'s in public places all for the cause, we'd drive through the clouds of burning oil to our worthless houses and we peel off our socks and throw them onto the floors. Our houses couldn't keep their value or our secrets, but at least they could keep our televisions out of the rain.

The Nihilist

He was on a plane again and now it was late, he'd missed a connection in Denver, and the west was dark and the big plane flew west in the night. It was half full and the people had spread out and the men were sprawled on three seats sleeping where they could. The steward had come by and brought him a coffee where he worked alone in a row at the back of the plane and then she brought him three packages of cookies and smiled and said, Knock yourself out. He looked at her and said, I'm not even on this plane. I was on the earlier one. He was tired now for the first time on his long trip, five or six cities, and the hotels and he had held up and then today the fall sun had laid itself across the hills of Utah in a way he recognized and loved and it hurt him, such beauty, and it seemed to be change itself and change had been a hard teacher for the man for these years, and he was sick of beauty and he was sick of change, but it didn't stop them from cracking his heart. My heart's cracked, he had said to himself so long ago now. And now, on the plane, he was just tired. Your heart, he said aloud. Who cares. Who fucking cares. It helped and felt good to use profanity when he was tired. It was lovely to spit ugly questions full of profanity when you were tired. The plane was roaring its whisper and he didn't even care now. He had wanted to get home for some reason and now he would get there and who cared. He was smiling with his new nihilism. He was quite the nihilist. Oh, he could zero with the best of them. He could out nothing the heavyweights. Then his nihilism grew thin and he was simply alone on a plane far from earth. His nihilism was fraudulent. He twisted his mouth in a way he sometimes did when vexed and now he was vexed as a fraudulent nihilist. He cared about too much. He could marshal his nihilism for about five seconds and then the world came up for him, all the people he cared for came up for him, their names, and he was kept by the names and the faces of these people from going again to the litany of nothings. He wanted care in his life. He exhibited care. He was capable of it. Fucking care. He was smiling again, so tired. It has been a long day and he'd been careful in it. Something good had happened, he knew, more than one thing really, and he had it in his pocket. The steward came by with her big silver bracelet and brought him more coffee much too late on a Friday night for coffee, but of course. He's typing on a plane, drinking coffee and the woman was somewhere safe and sound. That was all he needed to know. Oh, my heck, the woman. He was now thinking of the woman in her pajamas in her yellow sheets sleeping and now his smile was the real smile, the one that fit his face like a sunset. He was on a plane again, and though it felt so much like the end of something in his fatigue, he knew with true gravity that everything would be all right.

BRENDAN, BORN AT EASTER

On Easter we eat a cake
Shaped like the rabbit
Who brings eggs to the children of this world.

We talk of magic as a jelly bean
Passes through my head
From ear to ear.
All things make sense in my friends' house.

The hostess excuses herself
To go to the hospital
To pick up Brendan, who is waiting for spring.

The guests' hearts stand in the kitchen
Round and ready as eggs.
Everyone is full with children.

Brendan passes through my head like magic;
My heart beats like a phone ringing at two-
thirty, and I smile from ear to ear
Like a rabbit.

Every leaf in Connecticut has come out to see
The future, as it changes colors.

Rabbits wait in bushes for the summer,
And deer are flying through thickets;
Their hooves are heartbeats
In the breasts
Of father, son, and dinnerguest.

Brendan passes through his mother like magic,
And lies like a baby for a while,
Dreaming of rabbits, one hand on his nose,
The other on his ear.

Don and Hugh

IN A CLOSE DARK SPACE, A MAN, HUNCHED OVER AND CARRYING GEAR, MOVES FORWARD, PUTTING HIS HAND ON A SEATED MAN'S SHOULDER.

Don: Is anyone sitting there?

Hugh: I don't think so.

DON CLIMBS OVER, AWKWARDLY, THEN HIS GEAR.

Hugh: I need the aisle for my boots. There's no leg room.

Don: They've made this tight. Is there anywhere for the gear?

Hugh: Not really. I think all the storage is full.

Don: It would be. How long are we on this?

ANOTHER MAN, LADEN WITH GEAR, CREEPS AND STUMBLES BY.

Hugh: You tell me. It could be only a few hours.

Don: Or all night.

Hugh: How'd you get in here?

Don: Volunteered. Somebody gave up his seat. Is there a steward?

Hugh: I haven't seen one. Did you eat?

Don: Some, at the luncheon.

Hugh: I could have done without those speeches.

Don: I've heard some speeches during this whole campaign. I'll be glad to get home.

MAN IN FRONT OF THEM TURNS: Keep it down.

Hugh: He's right. We need to shut up.

Don: Got it.

AFTER A BEAT.

Don: But tell me.

Hugh: What is it?

Don: Would this work on you?

Hugh: What do you mean?

Don: The horse. Somebody leaves you a big wooden horse.

Hugh: I hadn't thought about it.

Don: Would it work?

Hugh: Great big horse like this one?

Don: Just like it.

Hugh: I've got to tell you the truth. I'd want it. I like a horse. Definitely. I'd take it home, put it in the yard, show it off.

MAN IN FRONT OF THEM: Shut up, you wankers!

Don: People would admire it.

Hugh: A huge curiosity.

Don: That's what started this whole mess.

THERE IS A CRACK AND A CREAKING AND EVERYTHING JOSTLES.

Don: Some guy's found his new horse.

Hugh: My god. This trip is underway.

Don: Buckle your belt. This is a one way trip.

AFTER THE ANIMAL FAIR

I went to the Animal Fair
The Birds and the Beasts were there . . .

Let's concede that you were there at the moment in question. It had largely been an long uneventful day at the fair. The exhibits, while not extravagant, were satisfactory. You had been strolling for hours and needed a cold drink and a rest. It was warm and the air smelled of feathers and hair, and by evening you were tired.

Then there was a special commotion involving the elephant, the largest of beasts.

Let's concede that you were there at the moment in question:
You walk into the elephant tent, weary from a day looking at exotic things. The whole world has gone ordinary in your eyes, and besides you've been carrying a child in one arm for hours. You hear a noise, some loud noise nearby and see something. Fear jumps into your heart like poison and every corpuscle in your body constricts, including the little feeders of the optic nerve.

Are you prepared now to say that you saw the monkey leap onto the elephant's trunk? Where did he leap from and how long was he on the huge beast? Ten seconds? Could you see all this in the moonlight? Are you qualified further to distinguish the sound or the spectacle of an elephant sneezing? An involuntary act. Can you be certain that the elephant didn't act out of anger, envy, or scorn? And hurled the monkey who knows where? Are you now prepared to say what happened to the monk? Can you even guess the extent of his injuries?

Even the day seems a little foggy in your mind. You remember the birds of course. We've been over that. But what about the baboon? Let's back up for a moment. It was late; you were tired. The moon was playing tricks. Was his hair, and we'd like your answer now, red or brown?

Syllabus

There will be four papers in this course, three informal response papers to the text, and one research paper which will be on one of the selected topics. The research paper will include ten footnotes applied in the manner of the Sheboygan Style Guide available in the Department Office on the eleventh floor of Lincoln Hall. Any students who object to using footnotes should see me for accommodation. Any students with ongoing addictions to controlled and uncontrolled substances should plan ingestion schedules so as to avoid any awkwardness Tuesdays and Thursdays 1:30 to 4:00 p.m. in our classroom, the Agribusiness Cultural Auditorium. Any students with concealed weapon permits should plan on leaving those weapons at home. Students may carry concealed weapon permits onto the campus. Neo Nazi students need not see me. Members of the Student Society for Cranial Tattoos need not see me. Students on Rogaine, Viagra, or any of the local versions of Crystal Methamphetamine should see me for accommodation. Students who are currently being stalked should fill out the blue half-page stalking form in the department office; without that form, we can make no accommodation. Students who are actively stalking someone, male or female, should keep a notebook or a journal with page numbers so that this material could be used in the research paper footnotes (see above). Students who are active members of Spirits of the Pentagram or the locally franchised Satan Says discussion groups should see me so that we can make accommodations. Students whose family circumstances include long-term generational feuds and continuing sporadic gunfire from behind trees in the hills of their hometowns should see me for accommodation. Students who are ranking officers in community militias should see me for accommodation. Active members of the press should expect a B in this course. Tops. Any student with full brains should see me for accommodation. Clones, robots and students who are from other planets should see me for accommodation. Students who have suffered from Spontaneous Human Combustion should sit near the exits and select the purple fireproof handout packets. Any students who are related to the University president, the President's cousin who teaches in our department, or any members of the Department's personnel committee should see me for accommodation.

In this classroom open flames, flagrant sexual activity, and gambling with dice or cards are discouraged. A second warning on any of these could get a student a yellow caution in the suggestion folder.

Attendance is optional, but call in from time to time. All phone calls will be monitored. Let's have a good semester.

On those footnotes: if ten is too many, nine would work. Eight minimum.

THE BARN DOOR

Okay, let me think. The horse has run away. We agree on this. I don't see the horse and we know the horse is not in the barn. Either the horse ran away because the barn door was left open or the horse opened the door and ran away. A horse could open a barn door, believe me. I've seen some horses that could do algebra, drive, arrange flowers. The point is that the horse wanted to run away. There's something here that the horse wanted away from, and it could be me. Hey, I've been good to the horse. So now I'm closing the barn door. The barn is empty. No horse in there. But, it is my barn and a good barn. Who leaves a barn door open night and day? Somebody comes by, they'll say, "Hey, your barn door is open." It looks like what it is, an act of neglect, plus it can't be good for the hinges. So, yes, the horse is gone and I'm closing the barn door. In addition, I'm nailing the door shut. There's going to be no reason to open this door again. And I'll tell you for rock solid true, I've never heard of a horse that could pull nails.

He woke in his bed under the open window and the great volumes of sea air were still rolling into the room. He closed his eyes and felt the heft of the air filling the room. The air had been working all night while he slept and now he sat up and then stood in it and felt it polishing his body, and though he was slow to smile, he smiled. It was fresh and he put on yesterday's shirt against it and pulled on his cotton pajamas and went out into the little kitchen and saw the coffee already making itself. He'd lived in a world now of little kitchens, a long season of little kitchens and he preferred them. Last night after dinner there had been a moment when all four of them found themselves back to back in the space and they'd laughed about trying for a record, the room so crammed that he could not open the refrigerator, and they'd all just turned around and hugged in a group with laughter and his head on Susan's shoulder. Later, she had come into his room with a serious look on her face and said, You are where you should be. There will always be a room here with your name on it, and she had looked at him so that his eyes watered and showed him where his towels were, stacked there on the end of the bed. He loved the towels and being shown the towels, and he wanted to work to a place in his life where he would someday be showing someone else towels. He picked them up and held them in his hand.

Now, with coffee on the table, he read his notes again and saw that the things he had to do which had defeated him at times in the weeks before would be possible today and that made the coffee seem very powerful and effective. Well, good, he said, something needs to be powerful and effective. He had not been powerful or effective. He had been present and was working on obtaining some power, but it was going slow. Effective was miles away. He could take steps, but he could not run. He looked up from his coffee and thought now: let's go run. The beach was behind him a hundred yards over the dune and he knew he would take his body over there very soon.

There was a noise outside his window on the dirt road and he turned to see two children dragging their little floatboards through the crushed shells and gravel toward the beach. They each carried plastic buckets and had a large towel draped over a shoulder. They walked hunched down with their burdens like prisoners headed for the great gray fields of labor and punishment, and their crunching in the gravel was measured and without gaiety, but full of duty and opprobrium. Poor children sentenced to the beach. They walked without speaking and their heads nodded like weary horses late in life.

He too was sentenced to the beach and he must abide that verdict. But for now he was typing and making a list, a glorious list, for it was made of things which the man could actually do. Here's the day at your door, he thought. Stand up and open your arms.

BABY

Oh baby, I love you so much
that I call you baby
even though you're forty-one
years old, wait, I mean forty-two,
but baby, oh Baby, you're my
exhumation, my unmitigated intubation,
my excoriating ablution
and the garnishment of all my mortal wages,
my silver salver and my radish dish.
There's some other stuff you are,
Baby, and only some of it has names!
I've been exculpated by you, for sure,
and more than once, as you well know,
for this is love in which we are
amalgamated nevermore to become risibly
insinuated in our alloyship. Battlements
Will crumble, etcetera, Baby, and whatnot
until infinity and infinity double meet
at the corner of You and Me Streets
in a town called, say, Heartburg or Heartsylvania,
Or Babyville, because you're my baby,
and probably if there was that town,
you'd be mayor, Baby, and Baby Baby,
you could appoint me Poet
Laughing Laureate.

MY AMERICA SLEEP

These were the years when people's teeth were getting whiter. It wasn't noticeable at first and then, sure enough, their teeth were changing. They had been okay, for teeth, and now they were growing whiter. People were whitening their teeth, a little whiter one day, and then real white. Very white teeth. Bright teeth, so white it was hard to look. These were the same people, but their teeth were whiter. You would see them coming with their teeth, and when they spoke it was hard to hear for the whiteness. It was also hard to hear because people weren't talking to us. They were on their cell phones, of course, and that was private. When they spoke to us, it wasn't always great. There were threats. Some of the threats were elevated to orange. The threats had other colors. You couldn't go a day without hearing of the threats. There had been threats before, but not like this with layers of threats. People were worried and things didn't bode well. They had boded well before but now they did not bode well. You couldn't get away from the boding, and people tried for a while and then we all did what our neighbors were doing. We bought big screen TV's. These had flat screens and plasma screens and ambient light and high definition. We wanted flat screens full of plasma. We needed high definition so things would be clear. It was so great to put the big empty cardboard boxes in the garage and set these things up and turn them on. It was just a moment, but it was a good moment, although we didn't know if we should keep the box or what. When we turned on the TV's there it was: poker tournament. The battle of poker, the tour of poker, the championship of poker, the world of poker. With high definition and the little secret poker cameras, we could see the player's cards. They had two fives. They had Big Slick. There were nicknames. There were tells. Everything was a tell. They watched closely. If someone breathed, everybody knew what she was thinking. If someone held perfectly still they knew. A blink was a book. This was in high definition. Meanwhile, no one picked up our tells. We'd walk down the street crying and no one had a clue. We weren't bluffing. We were heaving sighs and clenching our hands. We were all in. On television, the green felt tables were spilled with chips, and the cards were crisply displayed. The aces, lonely and arrogant, the sneaky threes, the hopeful sevens, the busy tens, and the queens all buttoned up with nowhere to go. The queens looked tired. They were exhausted. They were putting up with this, but couldn't wait until it was over. Their sadness was crushing. They knew something and it felt like something we knew. A couple of the Jacks had one eye, but that wasn't it, some accident in the royal family. She wasn't even related to the Jack really, and our sense was that she didn't even know him well. He's not the prince; we knew that. He just sharpens his moustache and works for the family, maybe in the stables or around the castle. He lost an eye and talks about writing a book about it. My eye and I were separated in the following way. The story is going to be totally suspect, the blend of fiction and fact, the accident full of danger and pity. We want to believe it, but come on, it's Jack. We were tired too and we couldn't figure it out. We weren't sleeping, but we refused to look at that. We had forgotten sleep. It had always been hard to remember and now it had vanished. Macbeth had murdered sleep and we understood the magnitude of the crime. We had sleep numbers, but didn't know what they meant. It was hard to get the number right and so many were in code. What's your sleep number, we asked. We were tired and wanted answers. Instead we had Starbucks everywhere under the green sign with mermaid's face on the logo, and she too was tired and threatened and worried about her hair, and she too was full of caffeine and mocha, now there was mocha. You could put anything with mocha and people forgot they hadn't slept. Macbeth was full of mocha when he was active. He taught us how to act in one fell swoop. It was an age of fell swoops. There were no benevolent swoops or sweet, kind swoops. Or neutral swoops. Fell Swoops was a series on television and you had to watch or they came to your house and made you. They knew; what hurt us was they pretended not to. There were electronic records in the plasma that knew all about us, at least about where we spent our money. We sat on the couch watching the shopping channel and there were some deals. All we had was remote control. We watched the poker players. Someone would check and someone would come over the top. It was painful. We didn't want to go over the top. We wanted to go past Fourth Street and wait by the river, where the Queen lay sleeping in the grass after her satisfying picnic. There waiting by the river, we saw her for the first time with her eyes closed. The breeze caressed her face carefully. It would caress anybody, but she deserved it after what Jack had done. Just seeing her there under the willows, made us sleepy too. We hadn't been sleepy in years. Tired isn't sleepy. Threatened isn't sleepy. Oh sleep, you tender stranger, come for us. You've got our number. It's either odd or even. It could be a fraction. It feels like a fraction. We are waiting by the river. With our mouths closed, we can feel our teeth glowing. Oh love, we want to smile so much. We'd done this to our teeth and now we only need a reason to smile.

Part III

Why can no one understand the importance of coming over to the window?

Our job was to lubricate the time machine and keep it oiled,
but man, we just now found out we're being paid by the hour.

WORD GETS OUT

Today's the day. You read
the headlines. Word gets out.
They'll give him ten dollars and a new suit
and a gaggle of the old gang
will stand around the prison gates
in raincoats smoking Chesterfields
waiting to take him back
to the world.

Today's the day. You listen
to the radio. Word gets out.
As you crawl by the windows
in your house, the cars drive
down your street. You lie
on the floor and bite
the back of your fist.
Word is out now;
Things will be different in this town.

Say Hello to Copper Bob

This tale is as tall as a man on a horse
Standing in the wind on Devil's Forehead.
Ladies, let me say I could learn to love to ride.
We've come across the Devil's Sideburn,
Stepping through the tricky shale,
Above the Devil's Upper Lip and Moustache,
Where we stopped to let the sweat dry
And map our way to your sweet dale.
We've ridden all the way from the Devil's Shin Bone,
Two days alone, figuring to be here for dinner,
If you please, having crossed the Devil's Pelvis,
Where it forks near Devil's Rise and Devil's Falls.
We've passed Devil's Pass
And the Devil's Hairy Ass,
Pardon my language, Dears, (but that's
what locals call the Devil's Rear.)
Frankly, it seems old Satan climbed
These hills first and named them all.
God only got the sky and Angel Draw,
And that's two counties south,
Well past Hell's Gate, Satan's Door,
And Demon Portico. Further than
We'd like to go, just now.
So Hello! In a country where there are forty
Ways to curse a man and just three ways
To bless him, I hope you'll say hello
To me, and to sweet Copper Bob,
For he is the horse I rode in on.

My America Notwithstanding

It was the worst of times. That's it, no follow up. No: but this or that or on the other hand or yet or still or notwithstanding. It would have been great to hear: It was the worst of times, notwithstanding something or other. We didn't know what not-withstanding meant, but come on, it's wonderful. We'll save it for the name of one of our children, the nickname possibilities are manifold. We'll name the other child Manifold. But these were the worst of times. It was a relief just to say it. Worst worst worst. This isn't understatement, which is the name we're saving for our daughter. There was no understatement because we were on the bottom, we had hit bottom, we had bottomed out whatever that means. We're naming our dog Whatever so he can behave in any way at all and not come when he's called or come when he's called. So it was the worst of times. We were done – yet we hoped. Isn't that funny? We hoped and we longed. Especially we longed. We had longed forever; it was how we were made, but it had gotten us nowhere. It was only good to make us cry when the music was playing. We were rife with longing. Longing, which is what we'll call the baby. We'd lived with the hope for so long it was a ghost. It was a ghost from a yesteryear we couldn't even see with multiplier glasses. Oh my god, yesteryear. No, it was the worst of times, period. Period period period period period. Worst worst worst. We were the same people, but it was the worst of times. We pretended everything else even though there wasn't much. We pretended all over the place that it was not the worst of times, but we kept coming home to it. It was the worst of times. It was so bad that small accidents improved things. Any moment when someone spoke to you and asked something real improved things. But it didn't happen because all we had was irony. No one said, nice going. If they said nice going, it meant the opposite or the opposite double. Everyone was self aware and then aware of that. And of that. A kiss was not a kiss anymore. It was ten levels back, dried out until you could laugh at it. A kiss we'd say and laugh. Sometimes we'd kiss and look around to see who was laughing. And this wasn't real laughter; it was made out of something shiny and brittle which dissolved in natural light. It was a noise we made, one of the last, be-sides the sigh. There was still the sigh. It was the only signal we had that we were be-ing crushed. We'd kiss, look around, laugh and then sigh. It was a vicious cycle; there were other cycles and we were caught in all of them. If someone said they loved us, it was a warning and affected our stomachs. Our stomachs had already been affected. It had been an entire era devoted to our stomachs. Our stomachs ruled the land; they led us around and had no mercy. They didn't care how we felt and we didn't care about them either. We ignored them, huge stomachs which we pretended weren't here. People said there is an elephant in the room, and oh how we wished there were an elephant in the room. It would have improved everything. First there'd be the question: how the heck did that creature get into the library? It doesn't matter. There is no room that isn't improved by an elephant. Sit here, we'd say, and lean against him. It would be lovely, but no. They were in short supply. We longed for an elephant, the elephants of yesteryear, while we sat in the library and named our children. No act contains more hope than naming the children: Notwithstanding, Manifold, Understatement, Longing and don't forget the dog.

THE BOSS OF ME

This is just to let you know
That you are not the boss of me.

The cold wind as it cuts along
my bare neck at night is the boss of me
and this October is the boss of me
and Widefield Park where I met you
last summer is now the boss of me .

Driving a person in your car
doesn't make them the boss of you
or messing around in that car,
like they let you get their shirt off
and struggles of that sort, which are like
nothing you've ever known.
These things feel at the time like
they might make that person boss of you,
because you start thinking
of that person every minute when you are apart,
and your heart seems like it's taking orders
from that person, and your guts, your hair,
and your body get all different,
again confused about their boss.

But you are not the boss of me. Tonight
the moon is boss of me and McKee Avenue
and your house there is the boss of me.
It's cold in the late night.
Your empty driveway is the boss of me,
and your dark bedroom window is the boss of me.
And where you are tonight is probably
also my boss.

The Final Shark Story

We were worried all the time. We'd been worried from the get go. Who isn't? Oh my god, the worry. Then we got past the ugly incidents with the Mummy and the Mummy's curse which had been a tough time all around. During that deal, we worried night and day. They said, Oh the Mummy doesn't know where you live. Just go about your life. Well, the Mummy knew where we lived! Luckily, he moved slowly in all his dirty bandages and so we had time to move. The whole family! Oh, you've moved; he doesn't know where you live now. Go about your life. So I was restacking the non-fiction shelves at the bookstore; we'd finished putting in the new blue carpet, something for which we had taken a worrisome loan, but some nights I would accidentally drive back to the old house, and those nights I could see the Mummy waiting across the street in the scraggly azaleas by the bowling alley. We'd fooled him, but really for how long? He's the Mummy. You're not going to be able to hide forever. About this time, we killed the big shark before it could kill any more swimmers. We used our ingenuity to outsmart and kill the shark. We didn't blow it up, which you hear about, but we killed it and we displayed the big shark by hanging it by the tail on the dock. This might have been when the other shark saw us standing there having our pictures taken. We were only trying to help. It had everybody nervous, that big shark, and we were happy to help the community. Then we began seeing the next big shark fin whenever we went to the shore. We could see it swimming right by all of the bathers in a straight line after us. The shark was following us. Other people noticed this. They said, That shark is following you. This worried us, naturally, because we understood revenge. We still had the big red ring and the golden Ankh from the Mummy's tomb and we knew the guy who wanted that pretty badly. Other people said, That shark doesn't know where you live. That was true. So we went home. But it's funny about being home; a person still worries there. Then one day at the beach we saw the shark fin coming and we saw the shark splash out of a wave and we heard the shark say, I know where you live. Well, who wants to hear that? By now everybody knows where we live. Plus, almost no one comes into the bookstore and we have all the good books. When it gets quiet in there among all the beautiful books, I vacuum the new carpet and look across the street. I'm here alone every day. Maybe somebody will come in tomorrow and order ten hardbacks for their bookclub. I should tell you that we have a whole big table of gift books and a table of How to. Things feel right, but one worries.

In Dwindgore

I'm going to omit some parts here,
skip the sexual content, and jump
to more appropriate sections of my story.

This all takes place on the blue shores
of Dwindgore, a kingdom prosperous
and happy and entirely underground.

The brave soldier Kormos was hot and tired
and he sat heavily on the gray slate by Poldor Pond,
his proto-tunic splashed with Mook-dragon blood.

It had been a punishing fight, but now
Dwindgore was safe, except for the Gob Squads
that roamed under Dark Kirdo's rule.

Kormos dropped his tunic to the blue sand
and then his fun-belt and nopkonner. He
marched naked into the coolness of Polder Pond.

Sensing a disturbance, Chynorra, the hydronymph
woke and saw his muscular frame approach,
his legs sparked fire in her loinerama.

Kormos saw the ripples of her approach,
Skip this part, skip, skip
Her arms over his skip and jump to
when his lungs were bursting she
Skip, omit, skip skip skip
Omit jump jump and skip to
tumultuous waves breaking over
Skip skip jump to – no – skip skip
omit for sure, and then, skip skip
and, oh, skip skip skip skip skip skip skip.

ACCIDENTS IN THE HOME

– most accidents happen within a few inches of each person –

Slipping on a pair of jeans
Skipping lunch
Hopping in the shower
Crawling in bed.

Throwing hammers
Loading opened bags of poison
Lying on knives
Standing or sitting in a fire

Poking the tiger with a broken pool cue
Drinking from rusty containers under the sink
Juggling bricks barefoot
Roller skating on the roof.

Now that I love you, you must promise
To be careful.

MOTEL LETTER

Listen. I want you to know
That I promise
No matter what, even
If heaven is a motel room
Close to the highway
That I'll find a way
To write to you
Immediately when I arrive.

I'll open the drapes and
Throw my jacket on the bed
And before the door swings
Closed or I push off my
Shoes, I'll find the
Stationery in the drawer,
Dry and faded, waiting
For my pen.

I won't know what to say
Really, but it will be
Something like I'm okay
And I miss you. Things
That were always true
And you'll know by
My penmanship
That it's me
And by the return address
Not to write back.

Elements of Courtship

Bring your beloved food.
Bring food
And put it there
By your beloved.

Take your beloved to
The food. Go
To places
Where food is.

Show your beloved food.
Point to food.
Bring it
To your beloved

Move food
To where
Your beloved is.
Keep bringing
Food.

I decided that we were in the old firehouse after some kind of fire, undressing, and the feeling was the same old feeling, that is everyone wanted to get drunk, but we could not do that, so we undressed heavily and breathed heavily, each breath a full pint, and I sat on a stool beside the bed and pulled off my left sock and then my right sock, each sock like the weight of the day. "The feeling was the same old feeling," I said. "Everyone wanted to get drunk but we could not do that." Gretchen said, "What is it, Allen?" She picked up my suitcoat and tie from where I'd dropped them and she folded them with her dress in a pile of laundry on the chair. She dropped her slip and unhooked her bra, turning by me as her breasts swung free and I noticed them as I had everyday in our endeavors.

"Some fire," I said.

"Oh," she said and she smiled at me. "The firefighters had another fire? That's a lot of work." She scratched the bulbous side of each breast.

"There's a companionable air in the old firehouse," I said. "It's a coed facility and the firefighters were friendly and familiar."

"Firehouse," she said. "The old firehouse."

"After the fire."

"The men and the women had been through some fires," she said lifting her gray nightshirt over her head.

"The fatigue was palpable." I said, pulling up my old plaid pajama bottoms. "But it would be difficult to sleep tonight."

"Not really," she grabbed the bedspread to pull it down, but paused. "It was a small fire, Allen. Smoke really. No injuries, no property damage. How much did you have to drink?"

"Not enough," I told her. Now she was in the bed, her glorious head on the pillow the way I'd seen it five thousand times.

She patted the bed, our old bed. "Your daughter is married and on her way to Hawaii. You did a good job. You looked handsome making your toast and it was a wonderful party. The band turned out to be perfect and everyone had a good time. Did you talk to Trudy and Morris?"

"Was there a band?"

"Get in bed."

"I think I'll tour the grounds."

"Allen. Wendy is not here. She's married. You want to go up and look in her room again at the boxes."

"Those goddamned boxes. I'd like to get those boxes out of here so we could do something with that room."

"What do you want to do with Wendy's room?"

Now I was sitting on the bed and Gretchen put her hand flat against my lower back.

"You get eight or ten boxes in a room and it's a fire hazard."

"We can handle that," Gretchen said, She tugged on my pajamas. "Come on, get back in bed."

"They'll be back for those boxes." I said.

"Wendy and Jim will be back all the time."

"Is that his name?" I said. "Jim?"

Lying back in the bed was like falling. "His name is Jim and you love him like a son."

The weight of the covers captured me. I could feel the blood beating in my knees. "In the old firehouse the men and women sometimes shared a bed."

"Sometimes," Gretchen said. "It was a matter of policy."

"They lay side by side in big beds with twenty pounds of covers on them."

Gretchen turned to me and slid her hand onto my stomach, saying, "But they never touched under the covers, the men and the women."

"They were too tired," I said. "And there was morale to consider."

Gretchen rolled a knee over mine, climbing and she slid her hand down. She was now speaking against my bare shoulder. "But, there was a companionable feeling in the old firehouse." She held me now in a way that changed my breathing. "And the men and women took satisfaction from knowing that they had done what they could, and everyone for one more night was safe."

MAX WHO CAUGHT A CAR

"When I found out that one of my years was seven of theirs,
I started biting absolutely everything."
—Max Carlson, Australian Shepherd.

I'm now a legend underneath this porch
where old age has me tethered in the yard,
and every young pup carries his own torch
to me, the dog that caught a '60 Ford.

The story's known from L.A. to New York,
how I dragged the Fairlane back onto the grass
and chewed it up like so much tender pork.
It took me years to swallow all that glass.

And still these young dogs come to see if I
can offer any help with their technique:
they scratch and piss and bark into the sky,
macho doggy stardom what they seek.
I smile at their bravado, all that toil,
and then I sleep, as always, drooling oil.

The Neighborhood So Far

If my heart is a house
then it stands on your street
in the little village
where you are paperboy,
mailman, garbage collector,
water meter reader,
building inspector, vacuum
cleaner salesman, UPS driver,
yard crew, chimney sweep,
window washer, tax assessor,
magazine solicitor,
census taker,
snow shoveler, house painter,
voyeur, door to door
scam artist, vandal,
burglar, thief,
extortionist, thief,
burglar, thief,
arsonist arsonist arsonist.

ENTOURAGE

– from an invitation letter: what will you require for your visit? –

I will need an entourage
to get from place to place
A phalanx of strong citizens
Who understand the race

Goes not always to the swift
Nor the good, the fair or bright,
But to the one flanked always
by a group on left and right

Who carry all the baggage
That an empty mind cannot
And offer praise at every turn
Regardless of the thought.

Zebra

You are on my mind
the way a person
clings to a broken table
after a ship sinks in the open sea;
and the way a girl
in a swimming pool
clutches a volleyball
in her legs, bobbing
for balance, splashing,
her smile so smart;
and, I guess, the way a leopard
holds to the neck of a zebra,
the two animals perfect,
the spots and the stripes.

The Execution

**A MAN STANDS FEET TOGETHER FACING THE AUDIENCE IN BLACK TROU-
SERS AND A WHITE DRESS SHIRT BUTTONED AT THE COLLAR. IN HIS
HANDS, HE HOLDS A LARGE BLACK HANDERCHIEF <u>AND WORKS IT INTO
VARIOUS SHAPES AS HE SPEAKS</u>.**

MAN:

And the entire family of birds: the pigeon, like so, and the dove with all of its sym-
bolism, and the robin and its symbolism, and the owl, who says who or is it whom,
and is wise they say, and the pelican, heron, and stork. Oh my, the stork and its bur-
den. The eagle for which it stands or flies, like this, and the raven, canny and social,
watching us, but then all the birds are watching, even the chickens and this turkey,
long may he baste. Hummingbird, parakeet, seagull, and crane.

And the orchid and chrysanthemum and peony and rose which also is the rose.
Voila.

And the clouds: cirro-stratus and stratus cumulous, great dark clouds lumbering
around the humid planet constantly, carrying rain and shadow and housing the
exhuberant lightning which arrives before its announcement.

And music: the whole notes and half notes, and every-good-boy-does fine with this:
the treble clef.
And the wind acting as if it knows where it is going, acting as if it knows where it is
from.
And the ocean and river and waterfall, and the barrel going over the waterfall.
And the horse.
And the wheelbarrow.
And the Windsor Knot, so stately.
And the Four-in-Hand, so eager to please.

And love and first love. And second love. And pain. And right and wrong. Here's
wrong again quickly. And here is right. Let me do that again. Here is love, just so.

And now I am ready.

THE MAN QUICKLY TIES THE HANDKERCHIEF AROUND HIS HEAD IN A PERFECT BLINDFOLD AND CLASPS HIS HANDS BEHIND HIS BACK.

MAN:

And the dark. And the light after the dark.

THE REASON WE HAVE SCHOOLS

The reason we have schools
Is to learn to say Goodbye.
The word is ours in study, years on end.
Goodbye, our teacher dictates every day;
Goodbye, goodbye, goodbye, we try to say.

All fall we study notes: goodbye, goodbye.
We type the message out on white bond sheets.
The campus changes color overnight.
Leaves fly about our feet.
They're yellow as goodbye and goodbye red.
They fall through goodbye sunlight on our heads.

Winter we work harder for goodbye.
How's that, we ask the teacher as it snows.
Close, the teacher says; she's not convinced.
We practice in the gym and in the rink,
and still there's more to learn. It's all we think.
All winter long the wind howls our dismay.
We cough goodbye and bundle it in coats.
It's living in our minds now like a song
that won't go away.
We write a twelve page paper on Goodbye,
this is surely all there is to say.
We've finally got it down in black and white.
Nice, our teacher notes, but still too slight.

Goodbye we sing in chorus, Latin, math.
The trees goodbye to winter and grow green.
And now the rain wears summer's name instead,
and leaves are big as roadmaps overhead.
At night we walk the goodbye paths
We know the answer hovers in our grasp.

On our exam the question is: Goodbye?
We put our pen to paper and begin.

 At last we sit alone in this high room.
Our class is in its last and its first June.
We're learning how to make the future sing.
And finally know just how to say one thing.

 for Jean and Bill Olsen

SOUTH PACIFIC

We were at the Highland Drive-in Movie Theatre, six of us in my father's 1956 Chevrolet after having been to the Hot Shoppes and then cruising State, three boys and three girls and not one pair in the gang, out on Friday night, a lark, and we entered the drive-in on a boast with Murdock and Kent in the trunk, emerging in the rippled rows of cars, laughing, and saying, what is the movie? It was "South Pacific" which turned out to be a tough, serious story with almost no battles scenes or sex, the chaste shampoo scene and all the singing and the sociology. Dora Nunley in the front seat said, we've come to sociology in action, and Duane Rummen in the backseat said, Mrs. Prenderhaven could show this in class, and we were talking like that late on a Friday night so long ago. Against the tide, the movie got our attention, drew us in and there were fewer wisecracks and finally Dora Nunley slumped where she sat against the door and put her bare right foot up over the dashboard and pressed it into the windshield for a moment, just a stretch. The next morning my father and I cleaned the car and we both saw the footprint at the same time, and he stood up and went into the house and let me finish wiping things down. He saw the footprint the only way he could, I guess, as proof that there was someone else he hadn't seen on the island.

My America Coffee

These were the days when we carried coffee. We'd carry it to our car and we had cup-holders. We drove coffee around. Seriously, coffee was driven for miles: cross town, out of town, around the block. We were driving the coffee and then after parking, we walked the coffee over there. Mostly we took it to buildings and up the elevator and this was a hot beverage. We all walked with our arms out holding the coffee. Even people who before had walked, swinging their arms or with just their purse or valise, these people carried coffee. We wanted to be connected to our coffee. We had something in our hands and it was coffee. Very little coffee stayed in one place. Every day you could see coffee being transported by individuals walking. Sometimes we spilled the coffee, almost always we spilled it. Not the whole cup, but a good spill on our shirt or levis or just in the car somewhere, coffee. Spilling it on our levis was not a problem because these were the days when we bought stressed levis. They were the thing. They were blue jeans which had been stressed. Stress was part of the value. They looked like they'd been worn all over the place and not washed which is a kind of stress. They looked greasy and sometimes there were holes in the leg or around the pocket, little frayed gashes which made them expensive. In the stores these pants in their piles looked like the castoffs from some great mining disaster, but that was what we wanted. They looked like someone had folded laundry after the oil well explosion. We had all stopped working some years before and we were now buying blue jeans that looked like they'd been at work under something rough and greasy. We hadn't thought that pants that were stressed in this way, being torn and stained and almost worn through revealed that whoever had worn the pants before hadn't been a particularly careful or effective worker. In fact the stress marks on the pants looked like these pants had been worn by the most careless idiot at the factory, some guy who kept falling down and catching his pants on the little sprockets or some guy who sat down the whole shift and faded the bottom of his pants almost to white. We wanted careless idiot pants to go out to the party. We walked up to each other in feckless, crazy pants and we said, How's your coffee. Did you get room for cream? If possible we made room for cream. It was one of the last things there was room for.

No Really There's Something way across the Lake

There's something way out there across the lake
For real way over there. Look.
Come out here and you'll see what I mean,
By the lake.

Come out, walk out on the wooden dock with me
And I'll point out to the blue lake with one hand
And take your hand with the other so that those guys
In the cabin will see me and you looking out there,
To the trees way over on the other side.

In the cabin they won't know anything.
They won't know what I'm saying:

I love you so much.
And I have loved you for so long.

ARS POETICA

Hoist the steel table up onto the roof during the storm in the middle of the night. You'll need a pulley and chains. Your work should be strapped to the table with sturdy straps. Rain will be lashing you and you're going to get pretty wet. In the laboratory all of your gizmos will be boiling and sparking as they should. Move carefully up there and check everything twice, the straps and the electrical connections. You'll be able to sense the storm building, the lightning stepping toward you in the sheets of rain. Keep at it even in the dark. You'll be way up there and all soaking. This is all you can do. Go ahead. You'll be working alone. Get that big table onto the roof.

Biographical Note

Ron Carlson is the author of nine books of fiction, most recently *The Signal*. His short stories have appeared in *Esquire, Harpers, The New Yorker*, and other journals, as well as *The Best American Short Stories*, The O'Henry Prize Series, *The Pushcart Prize Anthology, The Norton Anthology of Short Fiction* and other anthologies. *Ron Carlson Writes a Story*, his book on writing, is taught widely. He is co-director of the Graduate Program in Writing at the University of California, Irvine.